Published by Scholastic Inc., 90 Old Sherman Turnpike, Danbury, Connecticut 06816

ISBN: 0-7172-7890-5

Printed in the U.S.A.

First Scholastic printing, June 2005

TALE OF TWO SUMOS

written by
Karen Poth

illustrated by
Tom Bancroft

Based on the Veggie Tales® video "Sumo of the Opera"

SCHOLASTIC INC.

New York   Toronto   London   Auckland   Sydney
Mexico City   New Delhi   Hong Kong   Buenos Aires

"What a day, wrestling fans! I'm Jim Gourdly from the Veggie Sports Network, coming to you ringside where we have just witnessed the unbelievable.

"Sumo champion wrestler, Apollo Gourd, has just knocked his challenger out of the ring with a single, crushing *belly bump*. This contest was Apollo's last stop before the final championship round with heavyweight, Po Tato. But all that has changed.

"In a crazy turn of events, an unknown wrestler defeated Po Tato in an unscheduled sparring match. His name? The Italian Scallion. The question on everyone's lips tonight:

"Who is this Italian Scallion?"

The Italian Scallion is actually a cucumber who wears a hat that looks like the top of a green onion. He is Po Tato's sparring partner, and long-time friend.

So how did this happen? Completely by accident.

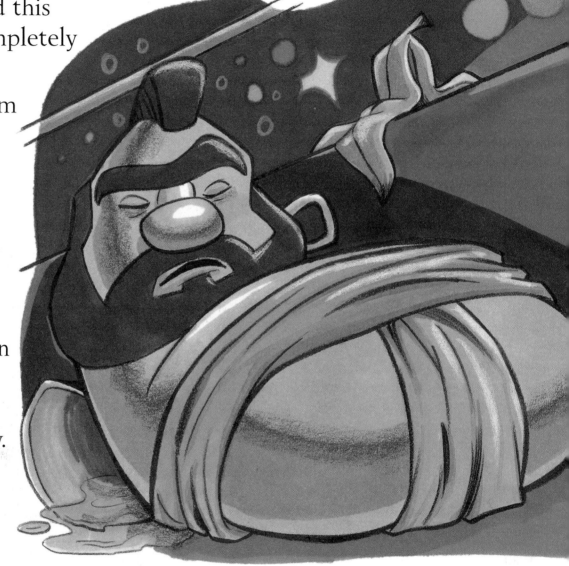

"I made him laugh really hard and he slipped on a banana peel and fell right out of the ring," the Italian Scallion explained to Po Tato's trainer, Mikey.

"Look at you!" Mikey scolded the cucumber. "You're always joking around. And now I've lost my best wrestler for the championship!"

"You say you want to be a champion Sumo, but the minute the training gets hard, you start joking around. You never finish anything . . . unless it's a punchline.

Mikey was right. The Italian Scallion was never able to finish anything. Just last month he promised his friend, Hadrian, he would fix his bicycle. But Hadrian was still walking his paper route, longing for the day he'd have wheels again.

"You're just a silly cucumber," Mikey said. "You don't understand that you can't replace hard work with foolishness."

Due to his silliness, the Italian Scallion would have to face Apollo Gourd in the Championship. This was no easy feat. No one had ever stayed in the ring with Apollo Gourd for more than eight seconds.

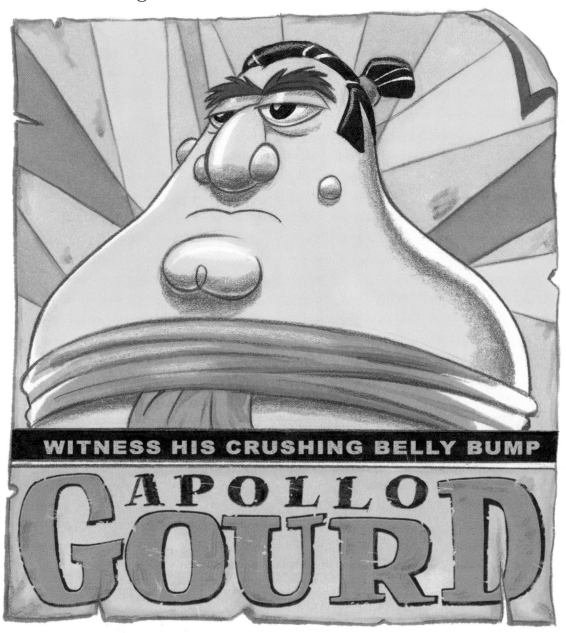

WITNESS HIS CRUSHING BELLY BUMP

APOLLO GOURD

"You have just two weeks to train for this match, Scallion," Mikey explained. "You'll never be able to stick with it and see it through to the end."

The Scallion felt a chill run up his spine. Mikey was right. He would never be able to last in the ring with the champ. **Unless . . .**

Scallion had an idea. "Mikey, if *you* help me train, I won't give up."

"Really?" Mikey asked. "No matter how hard it gets?"

"No matter how hard it gets," the cucumber agreed.

Scallion was sure he would be able to knock Apollo Gourd out of the ring. And the prize for winning the fight was a brand-new Tiger Bike. He could give that to Hadrian!

Scallion was determined to see this through. For Mikey. For Po Tato. For Hadrian. And for himself.

Each day, the training got harder . . .

and harder . . .

and harder . . .

Meanwhile . . . the champion did not take his new challenger very seriously. Apollo Gourd sat on his gym bag eating cheese curls.

"I do not need to train!" he laughed. "I can beat this Italian Scallion in my sleep."

Scallion worked like a champion. But working was . . . well . . . it was hard! Scallion became more and more tired. Suddenly, he stopped working.

"I quit," Scallion said. "It's just too hard."

"Look Scallion," Mikey told him. "Sometimes there's a good reason to quit, but not just because it's hard. God asks us to do many things that are hard. But these things make us better and stronger."

Mikey followed Scallion as he headed for the door.

"Most things worth having take perseverance," Mikey added. "That means sticking it out to the end. Perseverance, Scallion, **perseverance.**"

But the door closed. The Italian Scallion was gone.

Outside the gym, Scallion hung his head low. He had given up again . . . and it didn't feel good.

"Hi, Scallion!" Hadrian called out. "Look at the hat I made for show and tell! It's a scallion hat, just like yours. I'm wearing it because I'm so proud of you. You're a hero!"

Scallion couldn't tell Hadrian that he quit. He didn't want to disappoint the little asparagus . . . again. Suddenly he had a change of heart. He realized he had to finish what he had started. He couldn't keep letting his friends down. He couldn't keep letting himself down!

"Yo, Hadrian," Scallion said. "I've gotta get back to my training. I'm keeping my eye on that Tiger." So Scallion went back and worked harder than ever!

The day of the championship fight finally arrived. Hundreds of Sumo fans came to the arena, each one expecting to see the Italian Scallion get bounced out of the ring with a single belly bump.

"This is Jim Gourdly for VSPN reminding you that the first Sumo to toss his opponent out of the ring, wins the championship belt and the Tiger Bike.

"**But** don't get too comfortable folks, this match won't last more than eight seconds."

The bell rang!

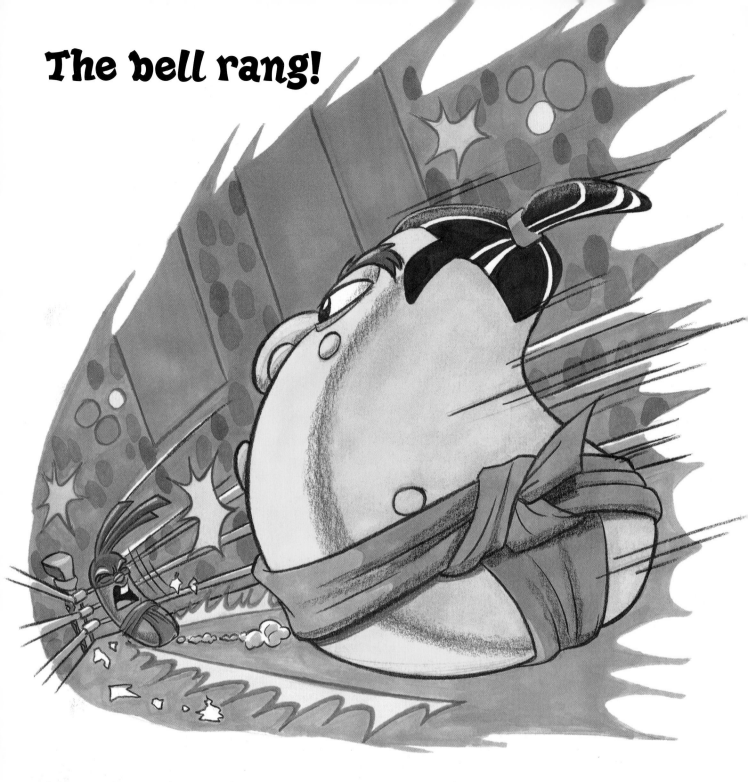

The Italian Scallion and Apollo Gourd charged into the center of the ring. **CRASH!**

They collided. Then Apollo pushed the Scallion toward the ropes.

"Scallion is in trouble already," Jim Gourdly whispered. "Apollo is pushing him out of the ring."

Just then, Apollo bounced into the ropes and flew into the air. He gave Scallion one of his famous belly bumps. But Scallion didn't move.

"This is unbelievable!" Jim Gourdly yelled. "The challenger is still standing. Eight seconds have passed, and the Italian Scallion is still in the ring!"

But Scallion sure was tired. As he looked around, his eyes came to rest on Hadrian, who was still wearing his scallion hat.

Then Scallion looked at the Tiger Bike and thought: *I have to keep my eye on the Tiger!*

With that, Scallion took a run at the champion and belly bumped *him*! The champion didn't budge.

"Mop the floor, kid!" Mikey called from the corner of the ring. "Mop the floor!"

Remembering his intensive mop training, Scallion ran circles around Apollo. The giant gourd got very, very dizzy, until . . . **THUD!** He fell to the floor.

"This is amazing, folks!" Jim Gourdly reported. "The Italian Scallion is pushing Apollo Gourd toward the edge of the ring! He's going for the win!"

But as Apollo was moved closer to the edge, he suddenly sprang back up. The two wrestlers took one final lunge at one another. The collision was incredible. They both flew out of the ring at the same time!

A hush fell over the crowd. Jim Gourdly could not believe his eyes.

"This is unbelievable! They fell out of the ring at the same time. This match is a tie! Apollo Gourd is still the champ. But what a performance by the Italian Scallion! He's a winner in my book."

And that's exactly how the Italian Scallion felt.
Even though he hadn't won the championship, he felt
like a winner!

"I did it!" the exhausted Scallion told the reporter.
"I persevered! And I feel **great!**"

Later that day, Scallion went to see Hadrian, "Yo, Hadrian!" he called. "I have something for you."

"You do? Did you win the Tiger Bike after all?" Hadrian asked.

"Nope. I did something else for you, instead."

"You fixed my bicycle!" Hadrian yelled.

"Yep," the Scallion said with a smile. "It feels great to stick with a project and see it through to the end."

The Italian Scallion learned that God wants us to finish what we start even when it's hard work.

HOW TO DRAW A SUMO!

STEP 1.

First draw a big circle with a little circle on top. They should overlap slightly. Then connect the two sides.

STEP 2.

Smooth out the side lines and erase your circle guides. Add three circles towards the top—these will be his eyes and nose.

Intersect the top two circles with a straight horizontal line and add smaller circles in the middle of each eye shape.

Now draw two horizontal lines across his middle. (These will be the start of his sumo belt!)

STEP 3.

Erase your guides. Now add two circles to both sides of the nose for his nostrils. Add another circle for his chin. Then you can draw in an outline of where his hair and top knot will be. Next, draw in the front of his sumo belt.

STEP 4.

Shade his hair, add those bushy eyebrows, his smirky smile, a few beauty marks, and you've got one of the most fearsome sumo wrestlers of all time—

APOLLO GOURD!

Veggie Value to Share

The Italian Scallion learned that God wants us to persevere. Can you think of a time when you also worked hard to finish what you started?